The Village

Bakery

Birdbath

For Anna, Iona and Holly,
who are also clever girls - AM

For my children, Jonny and Katie - SL

Text copyright © 2002 by Angela McAllister
Illustrations copyright © 2002 by Sally Anne Lambert

First U.S. Edition 2002

3 5 7 9 10 8 6 4 2

Published by Bloomsbury, New York and London
Published in England as *The Baddies' Goodies*
Distributed to the trade by St. Martin's Press

Library of Congress Cataloguing-in-Publication Data
McAllister, Angela. Barkus, Sly and the golden egg / by Angela McAllister ; illustrated by Sally
Anne Lambert. 1st U.S. ed. Lambert, Sally Anne, ill.
p. cm. Summary: Three inventive chickens find an ingenious way to escape from the two foxes
that intend to eat them. ISBN: 1582347646 (alk. paper)   [1.Fables.] Title. PZ8.2.M1225 Bar
2002 [E]–dc21 2001043981

Printed in Hong Kong

Barkus, Sly
and the
Golden Egg

by Angela McAllister

illustrated by Sally Anne Lambert

BLOOMSBURY
CHILDREN'S

Barkus Fox and his cousin Sly were bad news.

On dark nights they trundled their cart into town. If a window was open or a door unlocked they slipped inside and helped themselves to whatever they liked.

One night Barkus and Sly decided to pay a visit to the farm. "I would like a plump roast chicken for my supper," said Barkus. Silent as shadows, the foxes sneaked into the hen house and grabbed three chickens.

But when Barkus and Sly got home they were too tired to wait for a chicken to cook.

"There's a pie in the cupboard," said Barkus. "We'll put these hens in the shed and roast them tomorrow."

Now, the three hens, Biddy, Bluff and Tweed, did not
want to become a fox's main course.

"We're in with a bad bunch here," said Bluff, looking
around. "All these things are stolen."

"So are we," peeped Biddy, "and we're going to be
chicken pot pie tomorrow!"

"Pull yourselves together, ladies," said Tweed, plumping
up her feathers. "No one is going to serve us with cream
sauce. There must be some way to escape."

Biddy, Bluff and Tweed explored the shed. The door and window were bolted fast.

"There's no way out," cried Biddy. "We might as well start plucking our own feathers."

But Tweed had found a dusty box.

It was full of golden knives and forks.

"TREASURE!" gasped Bluff. Tweed tugged out a little ladle.

"Hmm, this gives me an idea," she said. "Ladies, let's build a nest."

The next evening Sly came down to the shed to fetch a chicken
for supper. When he saw Biddy sitting on the nest he growled.

"What's all this?" he asked.

"Don't touch her!" said Tweed. "She's going to lay an egg."

"Then we'll have YOU for supper and the egg for breakfast,"
Sly chuckled.

"But you won't want to eat this egg," said Tweed bravely.
"It's a golden egg."

Sly bent close. "Did you say 'golden'? Who else knows about this?"

"No one," replied Tweed. "But if you eat one of us she'll be so upset that she won't lay."

Sly looked suspiciously at the chickens. "All right, I'll leave you tonight and come back tomorrow. But if I find you've been tricking me there will be TERRIBLE TROUBLE!" and he snapped his hungry jaws.

Then snatching up an old boot that was lying on the floor he locked the shed behind him.

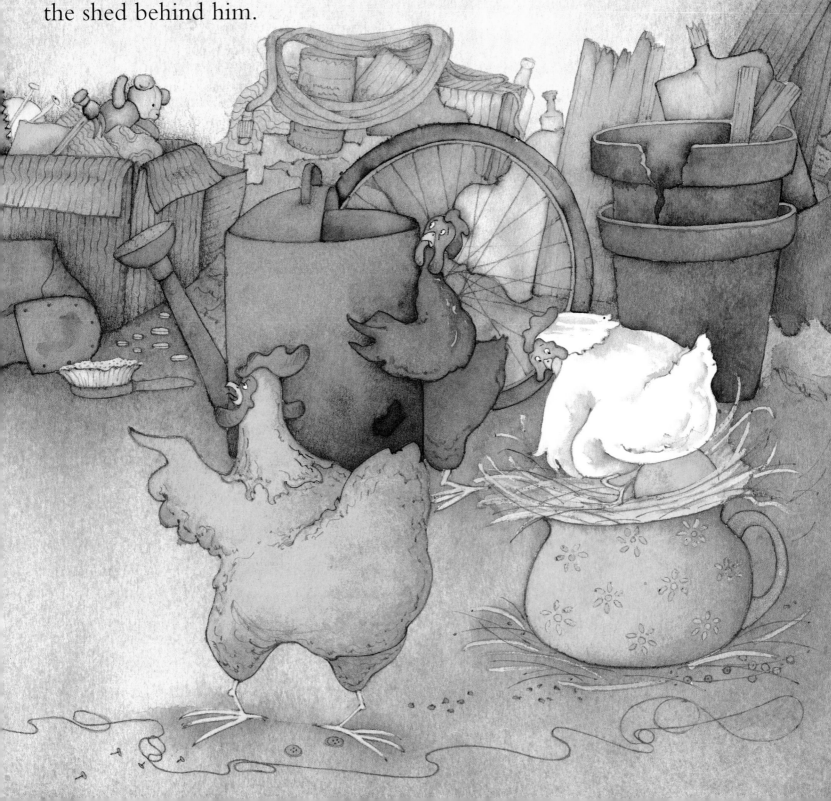

At supper time Sly made a stew, with some leather cut from the boot.

"That chicken was a tough old bird," said Barkus as he wiped his whiskers.

"Oh, do you think so, cousin?" said Sly. "I must have overcooked it."

As the two foxes sat by the fire Sly dreamed of the life he would lead when he'd sold the golden egg.

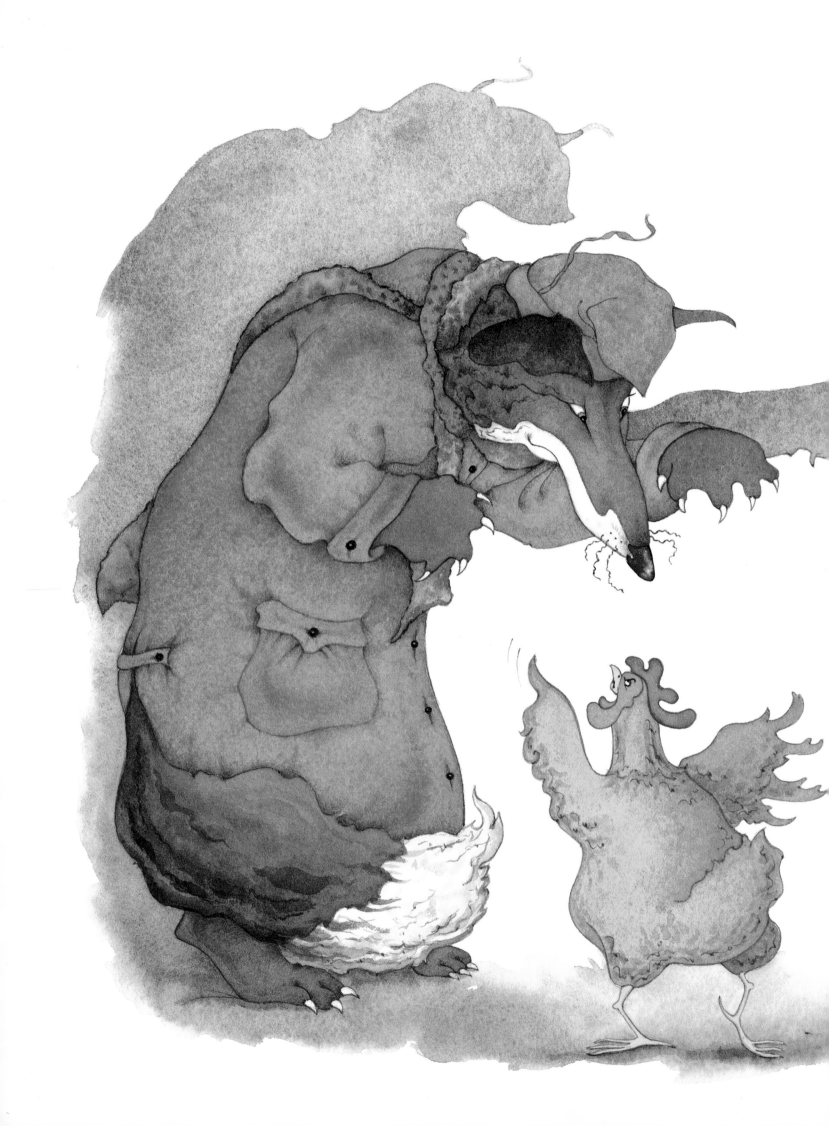

The following night Sly hurried to the shed. Sure enough Tweed lifted Biddy's feathers and there glinted the golden ladle.

Sly gasped. "Give it to me!" he said. But Tweed stood bravely between him and the nest.

"You cannot have it," she said. "You must let it hatch, for the chick from a golden egg will lay golden eggs herself one day."

Now, Sly was a bad fox. He had no intention of sharing such a fortune with his cousin. He made another boot stew and served it up to Barkus with a sweet smile.

"Ugh!" said Barkus as he pulled a bootlace out of his teeth.

"Oh! That's where it went," said Sly.

But the bootlace made Barkus suspicious. He went down to the shed where Tweed repeated her story about the golden egg.

"So, Sly has been tricking me!" growled Barkus.

"He plans to steal away with us," stuttered Tweed, "as soon as the chick has hatched."

"Not if I get it first!" said Barkus and he stalked off angrily.

When Barkus had gone Biddy and Bluff flapped around in a panic.
"Now we'll come to a TERRIBLE end," they squawked.

"Keep calm, ladies," said Tweed. "My plan is foolproof, you'll see."

The following night Sly returned to look at the egg. Tweed saw his greedy eyes glint. "It will grow much bigger if the mother eats plum cake," she said.

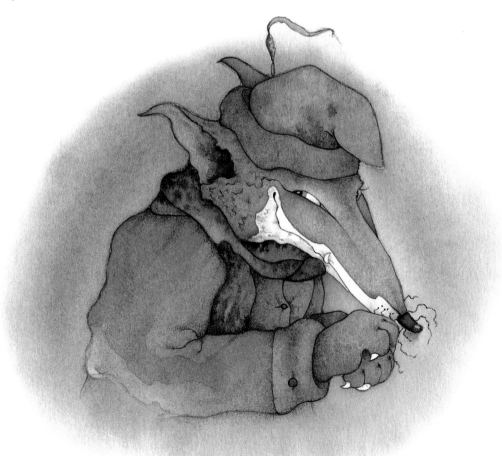

So, later that night, while Barkus was busy stealing a birdbath, Sly slipped into the bakery.

When the plum cake arrived Tweed said, "Don't eat too much, ladies. This cake has a job to do."

Tweed turned the cake upside down and told the others to peck away until it was quite hollow. Then she hid Biddy and the ladle underneath.

"Now, squawk for all you're worth!" she said to Bluff and the two hens shrieked together!

The first to come running was Sly.

"They've gone! They've gone!" cried Tweed.

Sly searched every inch of the shed, throwing things about in a rage.

But he never thought to look under the cake.

"Barkus, the fiend!" he cried. "Which way did he go?"

"Over the hill," wailed Tweed. "Oh my!"

Sly ran off cursing down the road.

Moments later Barkus dashed in. "What's going on?"
he cried, seeing the door open.

"The broody hen and the golden egg gone, gone to be sold
in town!" cried Tweed.

"I'll catch that scoundrel, Sly!" roared Barkus and he ran
off down the road.

Now the chickens could make their escape. But first they put the knives and forks into a sack and loaded it onto Sly's cart.

"We're going to return this treasure," said Tweed. "Now push!"

As the cart set off down the hill towards the farm Tweed dropped a trail of knives and forks behind them.

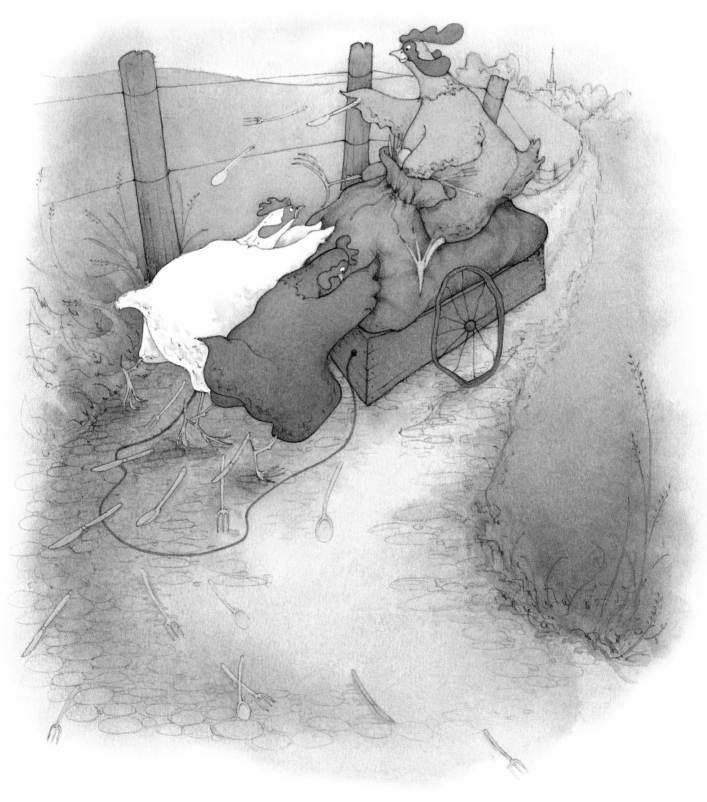

Later that morning as the three hens pecked happily in their yard the farmer followed the trail of cutlery and found all the foxes' loot. Everything was returned to the people of the town.

The foolish foxes never returned, and, although they talked of nothing else, they never, ever again saw a golden egg.

Farm House

Hen House

Barkus and
Sly's House

The
Shed